For EveryONE to Share

For Amy, Daniel, and Kate

— G.L.

For my beautiful daughter, Chloe

— D.H.

ISBN-13: 978-0-545-02217-0
ISBN-10: 0-545-02217-7

For EveryONe to Share

Gillian Lobel • Daniel Howarth

Little Mouse was fast asleep in his soft, cozy nest.
It was so warm, snuggled next to his mother and his six
brothers and sisters. Suddenly, his nose tickled. . . .
"Achoo!" said Little Mouse.

He did a big stretch, from his tiny pink nose
to his long tail. Little Mouse scrambled out
of his nest. All around him it was dark and dim.
But far away, he saw something different.
Something that made his eyes
water for a moment.

What was it?

Little Mouse pattered along
a leafy tunnel. Strange
smells tickled his nose. His
whiskers quivered with excitement.

And suddenly he was there — there in the big brightness.

Curious, he tiptoed into the daylight. . . .

And he saw — a tiny fat creature, dressed in a furry coat
of black and gold! He buzzed loudly in Little Mouse's ears.
"Who are you?" cried Little Mouse. "Please tell me your name!"
The furry creature buzzed even louder.
"I'm a **bee**, Little Mouse!"
And he flew away and . . .

. . . landed on something yellow and shining.
"Don't go," squeaked Little Mouse.
"Please tell me what you're sitting on!"

"This is a **flower**, Little Mouse," buzzed the bee.
And he climbed right into the heart of the flower to sip his breakfast.
"Bee, flower," murmured Little Mouse. "What a wonderful place this is!"

Little Mouse felt something soft and lovely on his back, and lifted his eyes. Far, far above him was a glowing ring of light! It shone on his ears and toes, and warmed them.
"Please tell me, Buzzy Bee, who is that?"
Little Mouse pointed high into the sky.

"That's the **sun**, Little Mouse —
the blessed sun! And she lives in the **bright blue sky**."
"Bee, flower, sun, and bright blue sky," murmured Little
Mouse. "And what is that, Buzzy Bee, please tell me. . . ."

But Buzzy Bee had buzzed away.

Just then, something floated past Little Mouse's nose and landed
right next to him. She was as blue as the sky and lighter than the air.
"Oh, Little Sky," he gasped. "Please tell me who you are."
"I am a **butterfly**, Little Mouse," she replied quietly, and
a silvery laugh rippled over the flowers.

"Bee, flower, sun, sky, and butterfly," murmured Little Mouse. "How wonderful this place is!"

"And there is even more," said the butterfly. "Look!"
And she showed him the birds, who filled the air with music; the whispering grasses, the starry daisies, and the dewdrops on a spider's web.

"And now I must go," said the blue butterfly.
"Good-bye, Little Mouse!" And up and away she fluttered.

Little Mouse trembled with excitement.
"I will go home and tell everyone what I have seen!"

But Mommy Mouse was already looking for him.

"Mommy, Mommy!" called Little Mouse joyfully. "I have seen so
many things here in the big outside — a buzzy bee, a flower,
the golden sun, the bright blue sky, a butterfly,
the birds in the air — oh, so much.
What is this place, Mommy? Please
tell me, I want to know!"

"Why, this is the **world**,
Little Mouse — the beautiful
world!" said his mother, laughing.

And they trotted home
together happily.

"The world . . ." murmured Little Mouse as he
snuggled into his mother's arms. "The big, beautiful world.
But who is it for, Mommy? Is it a world for us?"

"Yes," his mother said, smiling. "It is a world for bees and butterflies
and flowers, for birds and spiders and grasses that sing.
And it's a world for us, too — it's a world . . .

...for everyone to share!"

Then Little Mouse gave a deep and happy sigh,
curled up into his sweet, warm nest
with his six brothers and sisters,
and fell fast asleep.